AMERICA'S NATIONAL PARKS
Interesting Facts for Kids

MARC FRANZ

America's Top 20 National Parks Interesting Facts for Kids Copyright © 2018 by Marc Franz. All rights reserved. Printed in the United States of America. No part of this book may be reproduced or transmitted in any form or by any means, electronic or mechanical, including photocopying, recording or by any information storage, and retrieval system without written permission from the author or publisher. For information, contact White Bird Publications, LLC.

Visit our website at www.whitebirdpublications.com

ISBN: 978-1-63363-336-0
LCCN: 2018957939

"There can be nothing in the world more beautiful than the Yosemite, the groves of the giant sequoias and redwoods, the Canyon of the Colorado, the Canyon of the Yellowstone, the Three Tetons; and our people should see to it that they are preserved for their children and their children's children forever, with their majestic beauty all unmarred."

- Theodore Roosevelt

Photo provided by Stephen Shelesky

Yellowstone National Park

Yellowstone was the world's very first national park established on March 1, 1872.

Yellowstone is famous for its hundreds of geysers around the park, but none is more iconic than "Old Faithful." The geyser erupts every 92 minutes on average and is capable of spewing water 180 feet high in the air.

Yellowstone has the largest, free-roaming herd of bison in the world. It is also the only place in the United States where bison have lived continuously since prehistoric times.

Did you know?

Yellowstone National Park is larger than the states Rhode Island and Delaware combined.

Yosemite National Park

Yosemite's spectacular scenery was largely created from glacier activity. Over many years, glacier ice slowly carved out the valley giving the park its "U" shaped landscape and smooth rock faces.

The rock face known as, El Capitan, is the largest exposed piece of granite in the world towering more than 350 stories/+3,000 feet above Yosemite Valley. It is also one of the most sought-after places in the world to rock climb bringing in hundreds of experienced climbers every year.

There are many beautiful and famous waterfalls throughout the park, but Yosemite Falls is unique since it is actually the tallest waterfall in North America.

Did you know?

At a pace of three miles an hour, it would take nearly twelve days to hike all of Yosemite National Parks more than 840 miles of hiking trails.

Grand Canyon National Park

The Grand Canyon is considered one of the "Seven Wonders of the World" with its canyon being 277 miles long and up to 18 miles wide.

The Grand Canyon was initially formed by the Colorado River millions of years ago. The canyon is still being shaped by the river today through the processes of erosion, which is continually changing the contours of the canyon.

The Colorado River flows west through the canyon roughly at a speed of four miles per hour averaging 300 feet wide and 100 feet deep.

Did you know?

The Grand Canyon is not the largest canyon in the world. The largest canyon is actually The Yarlung Tsangpo Grand Canyon in Tibet, which plummets to a depth of 17,567 feet. This makes it more than 2 miles deeper than the Grand Canyon's 6,093 feet. The Tibetan Canyon is also about 30 miles longer than the Grand Canyon.

Grand Teton National Park

The Teton Range is the youngest mountain range in the Rocky Mountains at only about 10 million years old, yet it towers at a staggering height of 13,770 feet.

The Tetons were created through what geologists call fault-block formation. This fault-block runs north and south for about 40 miles. The land that makes up the west block is rising upward (The Teton Range), and the east block is lowering (Jackson Hole Valley). With these geological forces still at work, the Teton Range is continuing to grow still today.

Grand Teton National Park was established twice, once in 1929 and then again in 1950. First established to protect its mountain peaks and the lakes surrounding the mountain bases. Then in 1950, when the adjacent valley floors, as well as the Jackson Hole National Monument, were incorporated into the park.

Did you know?

Grand Teton is the only national park with a commercial airport.

Zion National Park

Angels Landing is one of the most famous hikes our national parks offer. It's known for its spectacular 360-degree views of Zion Canyon at the top. It's also notoriously known for being one of the world's most dangerous hikes. The trail is only 5 miles long but has an elevation gain of almost 1,500 feet. With sheer drop-offs on each side and only a metal chain guiding the way to the top, there have been a total of fifteen deaths so far from hikers falling since the trail opened.

The Virgin River runs through Zion, carving and shaping the canyon. On average, the Virgin River removes 1 million tons of sediment, which mostly occurs during flash floods. The result of this sediment removal is the canyon continually widening and the river channel deepening.

Unlike the Grand Canyon where the majority of visitors view the landscape from the top down, Zion Canyon is usually viewed from the bottom looking up. A good example of this is hiking through the riverbed of The Narrows. The Narrows is a gorge with walls over a thousand feet tall and the river sometimes just twenty to thirty feet wide.

Did you know?

In 2002, the Olympic Torch passed through Zion National Park on its way to Salt Lake City.

Glacier National Park

Glacier's wide range of wildlife has barely changed since the Lewis and Clark Expedition. With the help of early protection efforts, the park has maintained nearly its entire original animal species since Europeans discovered the area. The only mammals that no longer inhabit this part of Montana are woodland caribou and bison.

Glacier National Park borders Waterton Lakes National Park in Canada. In recognition of the bonds of friendship and peace between neighboring countries, the parks were designated as the world's first International Peace Park and joined together in 1932.

Triple Divide Peak is unique in that the Continental Divide and Northern Divide converge at the summit of the peak, which can direct the flow of water to up to three separate oceans. This means any snow that melts from its peaks can find its way into the Pacific Ocean, Atlantic Ocean (by way of the Gulf of Mexico) or Arctic Ocean (by way of Hudson Bay).

Did you know?

There are around 762 lakes in the Glacier National Park, but only 131 of them have names.

Great Smoky Mountain National Park

The Smoky Mountains are among the oldest in the world, forming at around 500 million years ago. They are unique in their northeast to southwest orientation, which allowed species to migrate along their slopes during climatic changes such as the last ice age, 10,000 years ago.

The Great Smoky Mountains is one of the most ecologically rich and diverse temperate zone protected areas in the world. There are over 1,300 native vascular plant species, including 105 native tree species, plus nearly 500 species of non-vascular plants, which is more than in any other North American national park.

The combination of Great Smoky Mountains conditions, such as, changes in altitude, moisture, temperature, and northeast to southwest orientation create a range of ecosystems that support a tremendous diversity of life. This biological diversity is the staple of Great Smoky Mountains National Park. No other area of equal size in a temperate climate can match the park's amazing diversity of plants, animals, and invertebrates.

Did you know?

The Great Smoky Mountains are known as the "Salamander Capital of the World" with at least thirty different species.

Acadia National Park

Cadillac Mountain, standing at 1,530 feet isn't just the highest peak in Acadia, but also the tallest mountain along the eastern coast of the United States. In addition, from October 7th - March 6th, Cadillac Mountain is the first place in the United States where people can see the sun rise.

There is a rock formation in the park called Thunder Hole. It creates the sound of thunder when waves roll in from the ocean and shoot air and water up through the cavern.

Acadia is known for its mountains and hilly hikes, but an important part of the park's ecosystem is its series of streams and lakes that exist within the boundaries. In fact, 20 of the park is classified as wetlands. In each of these wetland areas, at least one rare plant grows.

Did you know?

Acadia was the first national park to be created east of the Mississippi River and is the only national park in the northeast United States.

Olympic National Park

The wildlife in Olympic National Park is abundant and rare. In fact, The Olympic Marmot doesn't exist anywhere else in the world, besides in the park. Another special animal in the park is the Roosevelt Elk, named in honor of President Theodore Roosevelt. Early on, overhunting nearly wiped out the elk, but creating Mount Olympus National Monument ensured that the elk would be protected and avoided extinction. Protecting the elk was so important that, according to the National Park Service, Olympic was almost named Elk National Park.

Olympic National Parks forests, such as Hoh Rainforest and Quinault Rainforest, are covered in lush green canopies along with moss and fern blanketed surfaces everywhere you look. This is because the park's forests get nearly 140-170 inches of precipitation every year. That's welve to fourteen feet of annual rainfall, making this perhaps the wettest area in the continental United States. The large amount of seasonal rain contributes to the parks' 3,000 plus rivers and streams.

Within the center of Olympic National Park rise the Olympic Mountains, which formed over 30 million years ago and are topped with over 300 massive, ancient glaciers. High above any of the other summits, Mount Olympus is the crown jewel of the Olympic Mountains standing at just under 8,000 feet.

Did you know?

Mount Olympus can't be seen by any surrounding city outside of the park including Seattle.

Arches National Park

Arches National Park contains more than 2,000 natural arches, which is the greatest concentration in the country. The number of arches varies because new ones are constantly being formed, and old ones collapse as time passes.

Arches National Park was formed from the combination of wind, water, and ice, weathering and eroding the fragile sandstone that the park is composed of. A salt bed lies under the park, formed about 300 million years ago from a sea that once flowed through the region. Debris that was later compressed into rock later covered this salt bed, and the combination of water and wind eventually formed the arches and other interesting rock formations that remain today.

To be considered a natural arch it has to have an opening at least three feet wide. Whenever someone discovers a new natural arch, they get to name it.

Did you know?

Temperatures in the park can fluctuate as much as fifty degrees in a single day.

Denali National Park

Denali National Park is home to the tallest peak in North America, Denali. Denali translates from the language of the Athabascan tribe as "The High One" with its towering peak standing at 20,320 feet above sea level. Denali is known for its extreme weather with temperatures as low as -75.5° F and wind chills as low as -118.1° F recorded by an automated weather station located at 18,733 feet.

The only amphibian in Denali National Park is a type of Alaskan wood frog. It's different than other frogs due to its evolutionary adaptation that allows it to survive the parks harsh winters by letting itself slowly freeze its organs and thaw out in the spring. The frogs don't breathe, and their hearts don't beat, yet they survive in temperatures down to 10° F.

In a typical year, 1,300 people try to climb Denali. An estimated 32,000 climbers have attempted Denali with only about a fifty percent success rate. One in 200 climbers who attempt to climb the mountain dies trying.

Did you know?

There is a distinction between measuring "highest" and "tallest" when discussing mountain size. The highest mountain is determined by measuring a mountain's highest point above sea level. The tallest mountain is measured from base to summit. Using that measurement, Denali is actually taller than Mount Everest, rising 18,000 feet from its base, while Everest is only 12,000 feet.

Joshua Tree National Park

Joshua Tree National Park is popular with rock climbers. So popular that there are over 8,000 rock climbing routes in the park. The routes are typically short, because the rocks are rarely more than 230 feet in height.

Joshua Tree National Park is on the Pacific Flyway, which results in more than 240 species of birds living and migrating through the park. Many of the migratory birds live in nearby mountains and visit the park to escape heavy winter snows elsewhere.

The most well-known feature of the park, and the feature for which the park is named, is the Joshua tree. The Joshua tree isn't actually a tree at all or even a cactus, but a Yucca brevifolia. The giant short-leaved yucca plant is a member of the agave family. The yuccas in the park may grow as high as forty-feet, and the trunks may reach four-feet in diameter. It's difficult to determine the age of the plants since they don't have growth rings like real trees, but some are believed to reach almost 1,000 years old.

Did you know?

Joshua Tree National Park's oldest rocks date back to 1.7 billion years old.

Sequoia National Park

Sequoia National Park is home to the largest tree in the world, the General Sherman Tree. It is located in the Giant Forest standing at a massive height of 275 feet.

Sequoia National Park doesn't just have the largest, but also the oldest trees on the planet. Many of the giant trees average around the age of 500 to 1,500 years old, but can live up to 3,000 years old.

Giant Sequoias have a natural resistance to fire. They have thick bark that can often protect them from burning down. The species actually needs fire to germinate. The trees' pinecones will only open when subject to intense heat. Fire is also responsible for the way Sequoias grow in almost perfectly straight lines. When a tree burns and falls to the ground, the soil underneath becomes enriched with minerals from the tree, creating a narrow strip of especially fertile ground.

Did you know?

The seed of a giant Sequoia tree is only about the size of a piece of oatmeal.

Rocky Mountain National Park

The Continental Divide Scenic Trail runs through the park. It runs along sections of the actual Great Divide. The Great Divide is the invisible border atop the Rocky Mountains that determines whether water runs east to the Atlantic or west to the Pacific. It splits the park into its eastern and western sections.

The headwaters of the Colorado River begin deep within the park's boundaries.

Rocky Mountain National Park is home to the highest continuous paved road in the United States. The Trail Ridge Road runs forty-eight miles between Grand Lake and Estes Park with a maximum height at 12,183 feet (two miles above sea level). Although construction started in 1929, the road wasn't fully paved until the early part of 1940 because of an off-and-on construction schedule largely due to high elevation weather conditions.

Did you know?

The first female nature guides in America were trained and licensed in Rocky Mountain National Park.

Everglades National Park

The Everglades is the only North American subtropical preserve. It contains the largest subtropical wetland ecosystem in North America, which includes seventy-three threatened or endangered species.

The Everglades is the only place in the world where the American Alligator and American Crocodile co-exist in the wild.

Everglades National Park is often described as a swamp or forested wetland, when actually the Everglades is a very slow-moving river.

Did you know?

One out of every three Floridians (eight-million people) relies on the Everglades for their water supply.

Bryce Canyon National Park

The rock pillars found in the park are called "hoodoos." The park has the largest collection of hoodoos in the world. They range in size from 5 - 200 feet tall. The iconic rock formation is created a couple different ways. In the winter, melting snow seeps into the cracks of the rocks and freezes. When the water freezes it expands, widening and opening cracks in the rocks, breaking them apart. This process is referred to as frost wedging. In addition, heavy rainstorms during the summer months sculpt the hoodoos through the process of erosion.

Despite being named Bryce Canyon, the park isn't a canyon at all. Bryce is actually a natural amphitheater. On a clear day at the top of the park, visitors can see for a distance of nearly 200 miles.

Bryce Canyon National Park has one of the darkest skies in the United States. Far from the light pollution of civilization, the night sky at Bryce is so dark that 7,500 stars are visible on a moonless night. In most other places in the United States, it is common to see only around 2,500 stars. Bryce's night sky is so dark that visitors can see the Milky Way span from one horizon to the other.

Did you know?

Bryce Canyon National Park's sky isn't just dark, but also so clear that at night Venus and Jupiter are bright enough to cast a shadow.

Big Bend National Park

The Rio Grande forms a close to 2,000-mile natural border between the United States and Mexico. Big Bend National Park covers 250 miles of that distance.

Big Bend National Park contains the Chisos Mountain Range, making it the only park to have an entire mountain range within its borders.

Big Bend National Park has at least 450 species of birds that inhabit the park, which is more than any other national park in the United States.

Did you know?

Big Bend National Park's boundaries protect the largest amount of Chihuahuan Desert topography (physical features) and ecology (organisms) in the United States.

Hawaii Volcanoes National Park

Hawaii Volcanoes National Park is located on the island of Hawaii. The park is home to the two volcanoes, Mauna Loa and Kilauea. Mauna Loa is the most massive subaerial volcano in the entire world. Kilauea is considered to be one of the most active volcanoes in the world

Kilauea's pumps out its flow of lava at an average rate of 800-1,300 gallons per second. Because of this, more than 500 acres of new land have been added to the island of Hawaii since Kilauea first erupted on January 3, 1983, and has been continuously erupting ever since.

Mauna Loa and Mauna Kea volcanoes were once ice-capped with glaciers millions of years ago. Today, the two volcanoes still have high altitude storms that can occur without warning. This results in severe winter conditions, including blizzards, high winds, and whiteouts.

Did you know?

Sea turtles are the only native reptile to the island of Hawaii and live in and around the national park in abundance.

Badlands National Park

The physical features in Badlands National Park are largely made of sedimentary rock. The surrounding rivers contribute greatly to the parks erosion. Some parts of the park are eroding at a rate of 1 inch per year. Because of this, it is easy to detect the geological history of the area through the different colored layers of rock visible in the hillsides. Eventually, wind and water will wear down the entire Badlands until the area becomes flat.

In Badlands National Park, fossils of prehistoric creatures, such as saber-toothed cats, rhinoceroses, and prehistoric camels have been found, dating back thirty-million years.

At one time the Badlands were under water. This was discovered after bones of extinct creatures were found there, including turtle shells and seashells.

Did you know?

Badlands National Park's grasslands encompass the largest protected mixed-grass prairie in the United States.

US Virgin Islands National Park

One of the Virgin Islands National Park's most popular attractions is Trunk Bay. It is continually ranked as one of the most beautiful beaches in the world. Trunk Bay also attracts people with its underground trail for snorkeling through the coral that surrounds the bay area.

There are seven sea turtle species found around the world. Of those seven, three are found in the Virgin Islands National Park. With that being said, the turtles are common in the park, but they're usually only found in the water. They do come ashore to nest at certain times of the year though. The hawksbill turtles and green turtles are the most common, while the leatherback turtles are rarely seen.

The Virgin Islands National Park doesn't just protect the surrounding tropical forest. It also protects and preserves 12,708 acres of submerged marine habitat supporting a diverse and complex system of coral reefs and tropical fish.

Did you know?

The only mammal species native to Virgin Islands National Park are the bats. Other animals that can be found in the park or surrounding regions are not native to the Virgin Islands and were brought by settlers and later inhabitants.

Bison

Found in:
- Yellowstone
- Grand Canyon
- Grand Teton
- Badlands

Mule Dear

Found in:
- Yellowstone
- Yosemite
- Grand Canyon
- Grand Teton
- Zion
- Arches
- Sequoia
- Rocky Mountain
- Big Bend
- Badlands

Mountain Lion

Found in:
  Yellowstone
  Yosemite
  Grand Canyon
  Grand Teton
  Zion
  Glacier
  Arches
  Sequoia
  Rocky Mountain
  Bryce Canyon
  Big Bend

Wolf

Found in:
- Yellowstone
- Grand Teton
- Glacier
- Olympica
- Denali

Fox

Found in:
- Yellowstone
- Yosemite
- Grand Canyon
- Grand Teton
- Zion
- Glacier
- Great Smoky Mountains
- Acadia
- Olympic
- Arches
- Denali
- Joshua Tree
- Sequoia
- Rocky Mountain
- Everglades
- Bryce Canyon
- Big Bend

Brown Bear

Found in:
- Yellowstone
- Grand Teton
- Glacier
- Denali

Elk

Found in:
- Yellowstone
- Grand Canyon
- Grand Teton
- Glacier
- Great Smokey Mountain
- Olympic
- Denali
- Rocky Mountain
- Badlands

Black Bear

Found in:
- Yellowstone
- Yosemite
- Grand Canyon
- Grand Teton
- Glacier
- Great Smoky Mountains
- Olympic
- Denali
- Sequoia
- Rocky Mountain
- Big Bend

Bighorn Sheep

Found in:
- Yellowstone
- Yosemite
- Grand Canyon
- Grand Teton
- Zion, Glacier
- Arches
- Denali
- Rocky Mountain
- Badlands

Moose

Found in:
- Yellowstone
- Grand Teton
- Glacier
- Acadia
- Denali
- Rocky Mountain

Rattlesnake

Found in:
- Yellowstone
- Yosemite
- Grand Canyon
- Zion
- Great Smoky Mountains
- Arches
- Joshua Tree
- Sequoia
- Everglades
- Bryce Canyon
- Big Bend
- Badlands

Bobcat

Found in:
- Yellowstone
- Yosemite
- Grand Canyon
- Grand Teton
- Zion
- Glacier
- Great Smoky Mountains
- Arches
- Joshua Tree
- Sequoia
- Rocky Mountain
- Everglades
- Bryce Canyon
- Big Bend
- Badlands

"Going to the mountains is going home."

-John Muir
-Our National Parks, (1901),

Photo provided by
Stephen Shelesky

"When I was a kid I always loved being outside, whether it was playing sports, fishing, or just messing around with friends. I really got my taste for the outdoors in the Scouts. Camping and learning about my surroundings in central Texas where I grew up fascinated me. My family also took vacations all around the United States, opening my eyes to what the country had to offer, including our country's national parks. Being a kid, it was a bit overwhelming trying to soak in all the information within the parks we visited. I remember not having something I could take home with me, not as a souvenir, but a resource to look back at and learn about the place I visited, as well as other parks I might want to visit in the future. As I got older, and my interest in the national parks only grew, traveling through almost every one of them, I still noticed there was a lack of books for kids the age I was when I became intrigued with the parks. So I decided to make one myself. This book is to fill that gap and tell kids what I would like to have known about the parks when I was their age.

So get outside and explore our national parks today."

- Marc Franz

Photo taken on the way to the summit of Flattop Mountain in Rocky Mountain National Park.

Photo provided by Stephen Shelesky

CPSIA information can be obtained
at www.ICGtesting.com
Printed in the USA
FSHW011924281018
53281FS